W9-AKE-050

To Nicole Mandrell Shipley,
an answer to a mother's prayers.
And to Clint and Rance Collins,
the godchildren who have
blessed my life beyond compare.
LOUISE

For my sons, Clint and Rance,
who have taught me that
a parent's smiles and tears
are the most precious
of all of God's gifts.
ACE

To all the children
who will touch this book,
may your childhood
be filled with love.
LOUISE AND ACE

Best Man for the Job

Best Man for

Louise Mandrell and Ace Collins

Children's Holiday Adventure Series
Volume 10

THE SUMMIT GROUP
1227 West Magnolia, Suite 500, Fort Worth, Texas 76104
© 1993 by Louise Mandrell and Ace Collins. All rights reserved.
This document may not be duplicated in any way without the expressed written consent
of the publisher. Making copies of this document, or any portion of it for any purpose
other than your own, is a violation of the United States copyright laws.
All rights reserved. Published 1993.
Printed in the United States of America.

93   10   9   8   7   6   5   4   3   2   1

Jacket and Book Design by Cheryl Corbitt

LIBRARY OF CONGRESS CATALOGING-IN-PUBLICATION DATA
Mandrell, Louise.
  Best man for the job / Louise Mandrell and Ace Collins; illustrated by Don Morris.
    p. cm. – (Louise Mandrell & Ace Collins holiday adventure series; v. 10)
    Summary: Mitzi's father, heavy and clumsy and not her image of the ideal father, wreaks
havoc in his attempts to be a good dad until the true meaning of Father's Day becomes clear.
    ISBN 1-56530-039-4: $12.95
    [1. Fathers and daughters – Fiction. 2. Father's Day – Fiction.] I. Collins, Ace. II. Morris, Don,
ill. III. Title. IV. Series: Mandrell, Louise. Louise Mandrell & Ace Collins holiday adventure
series; v. 10.
PZ7. M31254Be   1993
[Fic] – dc20   93-311
CIP
AC

the Job

Illustrated by Don Morris

THE SUMMIT GROUP

A tired but enthusiastic Bob Williams watched through thick glasses as twelve girls took the field and warmed up. A hot afternoon sun baked the Texas soil, and there wasn't a cloud in the May sky. Bob had worked a long day at the office, and he hadn't even had time to change out of his suit before the soccer game. Yet there was very little that was more important to him than this game.

Rubbing his balding head, he studied his daughter, Mitzi, as she practiced her goal kicks. He was proud of this short blonde. She was everything that he wasn't: fast, lean, and athletic. He felt that the time that he invested in this team was worth it simply because of the joy Mitzi received from playing.

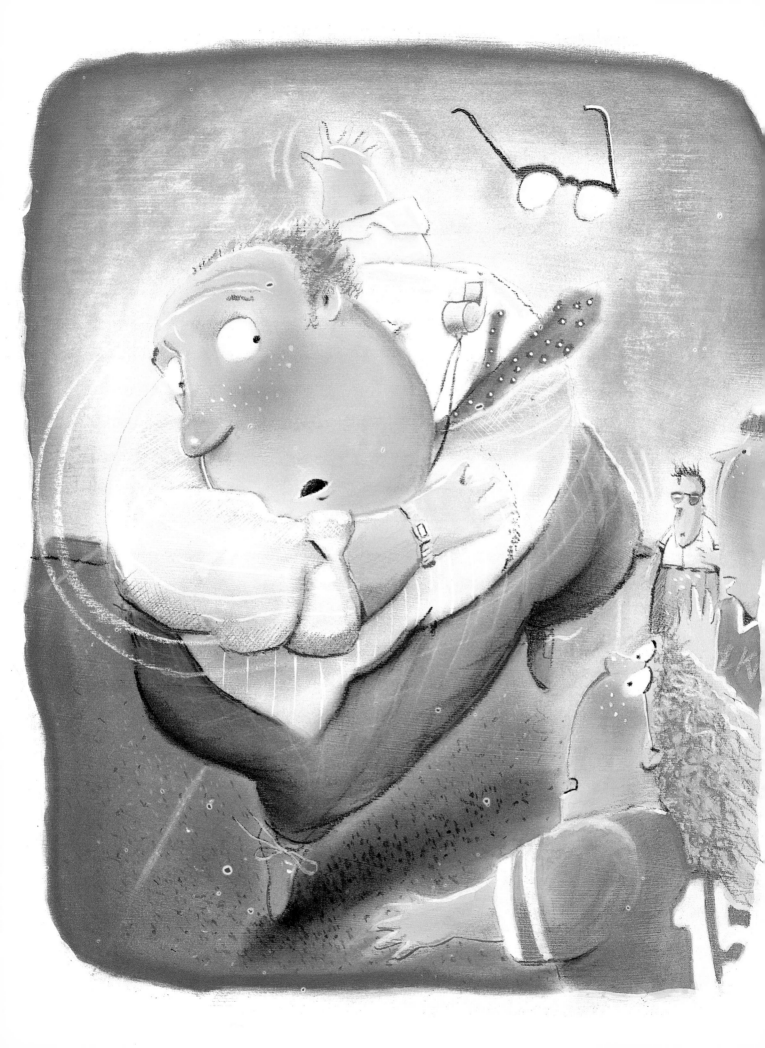

Checking his watch, Bob got up from the bench, took a whistle from his pocket, and blew it. Waving at his team, he signalled that it was time for their pregame meeting. As they approached, he tried to suck in his stomach and push out his chest. He was trying his best to look like a coach. Unfortunately, his efforts didn't do much to change his appearance. He looked more like a penguin than an athlete.

"Team," he began, "today the Sidekicks can take the city title. You have had a great year, and I know that you can win it all. All you have to do is play as a team. This is the moment we've been waiting for for three years. Now, let's go get 'em!"

Raising his right hand, he sought out Mitzi and poised his large frame for a high five. Bending his knees, he pushed his two hundred and twenty pounds off the ground. Launching his arm forward, he fanned the air, but in the process, he knocked his glasses off. Suddenly the world became a blur and Bob missed his daughter's outstretched hand by at least a foot. As a crowd of parents watched, the big man twirled in the air, a look of panic etched on his face. Having no idea where he was or what he should do, he simply toppled over. He landed on his knees beside the goal, and, before he could regain his balance, he fell forward, knocking the goal over.

As Bob searched the grass for his glasses, Mitzi turned a bright shade of red. A soft murmur began to circulate through the crowd, and, within seconds, it had become a chorus of laughter. Every fan and player was pointing and snickering at the Sidekick's coach.

Two hours later, as the team was having its victory dinner at Jim's Pizza Palace, Bob's great fall was the main topic of conversation. Mitzi was mortified. She didn't want to eat pizza; she wanted to go home.

Through it all, Bob Williams just smiled. His heart was too filled with pride to be embarrassed. His team had won, and his little girl had made the All-Star Squad. His clumsiness couldn't detract from that.

The next day at work Bob pointed out the team picture in the local paper. He told everyone at the office that the Sidekicks were the greatest group of kids he had ever known. He also informed anyone who would listen that his little girl, Mitzi, would deliver her award-winning speech at the P.T.A. meeting that night. He suggested that, if they got a chance, they should go hear her.

"Bob," his boss observed, "you just live for your family, don't you?"

Nodding, Bob smiled and looked at the framed photos that lined his desk. There were several of Mitzi; her sister, Marsha; and Dodie, their mother and his wife. "They are what makes my life complete!" he admitted.

That evening Mitzi, Marsha, and Dodie dined early, not waiting for Bob to get home. As they ate, seven-year-old Marsha asked, "Where's Dad?"

"He had some things he had to finish at the office," Dodie explained. "Because of the soccer season, he's gotten behind at work."

"Will he be coming to the P.T.A. meeting?" Mitzi asked.

"Sure," her mother assured her, "he's coming straight from work."

"Oh, great," Mitzi sighed.

"You act like you don't want him there," her mother observed.

"You saw him last night," Mitzi responded. "Everyone laughed at him! He's always embarrassing me. Why can't he be cool like Amanda McNeil's dad?"

Shaking her head, Dodie frowned, "Now, you shouldn't feel that way. He can't help it if he's a little clumsy. Tonight will be different. All he's going to do is watch you give a speech. What could possibly happen?"

Checking his watch, Bob Williams noted that he had just enough time to get from work to Mitzi's school. Jumping in the car, he pulled out into traffic. Just as he did, the light mist turned into a driving rain. Shaking his head, he leaned forward to try to see between the windshield wipers as they swept the water away. I hope I get there in time, he thought.

Finally Bob decided to take a shortcut on a dirt road. He had gone only a block when he felt a strange thumping. Realizing what it meant made him feel sick. He had a flat tire! Stopping the car, he opened the driver's side door and waded out onto the muddy street. The tire was flat, all right. He sloshed back to the trunk to find the jack and the spare.

Fifteen minutes later, when Mitzi took the stage, she searched the auditorium for her father's bespectacled, round face. But she didn't see him. Maybe she had a chance to make it through the evening without being flustered by something he did. Taking a deep breath, she began her speech.

At that same instant, unnoticed by Mitzi or anyone else, a very wet and mud-splattered Bob Williams sneaked in the room's back door. He watched his daughter from there, taking in every word, noting every expression.

After her speech, as the applause died down, Bob headed
for an empty chair in the back row. But he never made it.

His mud-covered shoes slipped on the tile floor, and
he completely lost his balance. One foot slid forward, the
other backward, and his arms shot straight up in the air.
In an effort to catch himself, he grabbed onto a large piece
of twisted crepe paper that had been strung around the
room as a decoration. The red, white, and blue paper

pulled loose, not just where Bob grabbed it, but every-where around the room. As he continued to slide toward a science awards table filled with caged rabbits, hamsters, and chickens, the falling decorations rained down on everyone.

And everyone, including Mitzi, stood up, and turned around, to watch in horror as the heavy-set man skidded across the rear of the room and closed in on the long, folding table. With a loud crash, Bob Williams upset the science awards table, sending the cages to the floor. Long-eared rabbits, nervous rodents, and frightened fowl

dashed in every direction. Children began crying over their ruined science projects, and parents yelled after them as they chased the panicked animals around the auditorium. The P.T.A. president sensed that she would never regain control that night. So, in an act of desperation, she was the first to hit the exit, followed closely by Mitzi Williams. As the two ran out into the rain, the woman glanced over at the girl and shrieked, "Who *was* that clumsy man?"

Shaking her head, Mitzi answered, "I really don't want to know."

The next weekend, Mitzi had to leave town and she was very glad to go. All her friends were still talking about what happened at the P.T.A. meeting, and a camp-out with her scout troop seemed like the perfect refuge. But then came an ominous development.

Brian Carpenter's father, an excellent outdoorsman who wrote for a national camping magazine, was supposed to lead the group on the trip. But at the last minute he had been called out of town to cover an important event. The girls had to go camping and spend a weekend in the wide open spaces in order to earn their merit badges, and they didn't want the trip to be cancelled. They looked everywhere for someone else to lead the group, but the only person they could find was Mitzi's father. This was going to be a disaster!

Despite Mitzi's fears, the first day and night went smoothly. They set up camp, told stories, and slept under a full moon and a clear sky. But the following day would not be so peaceful.

Bob Williams wanted to show the troop how to fly-fish. As he waded into the river to demonstrate, he caught his hook and line on a tree. When he jerked it back, the line broke. He lost his balance, and fell over backward. Landing in the river with a tremendous splash, he began shooting down the rapids. He struggled against the swirling water for almost a minute before he saw the waterfall. He frantically pounded the stream with his arms in an effort to swim out, but it was too late. The current caught him and pushed him over the ten-foot falls.

Meanwhile the troop members watched him go over the fall's edge in horror. They stared silently into the blue pool of still water at the base of the falls. Then they saw a

large blast of bubbles and heard a loud roar. Bob Williams flew up from the bottom, exploded out of the water, and fell onto his side.

Cheering wildly, the troop watched him dog paddle over to an island of logs in the middle of the stream, and signal that he was all right. Then he met his next problem. A family of beavers did not appreciate having the large man beach himself on their lodge. They chased him back into the water and didn't quit barking until he had made it to the shore.

The girls in the troop crowded around him, asking him over and over if he were all right. Mitzi's relief turned to embarrassment once she saw that he was safe.

After drying out, Mitzi's father built a fire and cooked supper. He forgot to stir the stew, however, and it burned. The scouts ended up eating damp crackers and chips. As she sat at the campfire chewing on a cracker, Mitzi hoped they could get through one more night without some catastrophe. Tomorrow they would be going home.

But that night a heavy storm system moved into the area. The wind howled. The lighting flashed. The thunder roared, and her father's tent collapsed. As Mitzi hid in Amanda's tent, her father, dressed in pajamas decorated with shamrocks, fought the rain and wind, trying to hold the camp together. But the tent and most of the camping equipment were caught in a flash flood and floated into the river. He spent the night sleeping in the van.

As the troop packed up what was left of the camp Sunday morning, Mitzi suffered her greatest embarrassment yet. Because all his clothes had been lost in the stream, Bob Williams drove them home wearing his pajamas – the green and gray ones with the shamrocks on them! It was bad enough that he wore them at home, but on the interstate? Her friends giggled all the way back to town.

For most of the next week, Mitzi avoided her father as much as possible. She saw him at breakfast and supper but spent most of her time in her room or over at Amanda's house. How she envied her best friend.

"Your dad is so cool," Mitzi sighed. "Everyone looks up to him. I wish I had a dad like that."

Amanda grinned and asked, "What did your dad do now?"

"You wouldn't believe it if I told you," Mitzi groaned.

"Try me," Amanda begged.

"This morning he was painting the second story of our house," she began. "He had just gotten up on the ladder."

"Let me guess," Amanda cut in. "He fell off the ladder."

"No," her friend whimpered. "He dropped the can of paint."

"People do that all the time," Amanda laughed. "My dad spilled a whole bucket in our backyard one time."

"Well, Dad dropped his on Reverend Bowers' wife," Mitzi sheepishly explained.

"The preacher's wife?" Amanda gasped. "Was she wearing one of her fancy dresses?"

"Yes," Mitzi groaned, "that blue one she's always showing off. And she had just gotten her hair fixed."

Shaking her head, she added, "Do you know what
tomorrow is?"

"Sunday."

"Yes," Mitzi agreed, "but it's also Father's Day. You
have a reason to celebrate. I don't. For me it will be a day
of mourning!"

Early the next day, the Williams family got up and went to church. Mrs. Williams sat on one side of her husband, Marsha on the other, with Mitzi positioned at the far end of the pew in a futile attempt to look as if she had come alone. As the congregation sang songs and listened to announcements, Mitzi couldn't help but notice all the other fathers with their families. If only one of them could be mine, she thought .

Anne's dad was the mayor, and Becky's was a former pro football player. They had reason to be proud. So did her friend Amanda. No one laughed at their fathers. Sighing, she wondered what she had done to deserve a father like the one she had. As she sank deeper and deeper into self-pity, she noticed Mrs. Bowers. She couldn't help staring at the minister's wife. She thought she could still see spots of white paint in her hair. How would she ever face her again?

"Ladies and gentlemen," Reverend Bowers said from the pulpit, "this is a special day, one on which we honor all our fathers. However, in attendance today, just like he is every week, is a man who deserves extra recognition. Therefore, at a special dinner this evening, our mayor will honor this man as 'Father of the Year.' This morning some of his biggest fans have asked me if they may share a few words of tribute. Ladies . . . ."

On cue Amanda, Becky, and Anne left their seats and walked to the front of the church. Standing beside Reverend Bowers, Anne spoke first.

"If this father hadn't taken the time to work with us over the past three years, we would not have had a soccer team. No one else had time to coach us, but Mr. Williams made the time for us. He raised money for uniforms, bought our soccer balls, and left work early just for us. His enthusiasm and spirit kept us going through two losing seasons, and this year we learned how to be winners."

Stepping up to the microphone, Becky took over. "None of us would have earned camping merit badges this year if Mr. Williams hadn't taken us camping. He doesn't even like to camp, but we had no one else to turn to. He fell in the river and lost his tent and most of his equipment, but he never complained. He taught us all how to make the best of even the worst situation."

Finally, Amanda stepped up. "I have known Mr. Williams all my life. His daughter Mitzi is my best friend. No father gives more time to his children than he does to Mitzi and her sister. He is always there for them. He never misses anything that they do. They are very lucky to have a father who cares so much and gives so much of his time."

As her three friends took their seats and Reverend Bowers moved back to the pulpit, Mitzi turned and looked down the row. The man she saw sitting between her mother and sister looked different now. She was seeing him in a new light.

"Bob Williams," Reverend Bowers said, "will you and your daughters please step forward?"

As the three of them joined hands and walked up the aisle to the middle of the sanctuary, the pastor continued. "This year we honor Bob, but not for being the smartest or the richest father in town." Reaching out and patting Mr. Williams on the back, the tall, deep-voiced minister concluded, "The worth of a father is not measured in money or fame. His value is judged only by the ways he gives his time and love. Here is a man who is a role model for all fathers."

Bob Williams watched in amazement as everyone stood up and applauded. The longer they clapped, the more deeply he blushed. Finally, when the pastor raised his hand and everyone again found their seats, Bob looked down at his two girls and smiled.

"Thank you," he whispered.

He then began the short trip back to his pew. He didn't notice that the microphone cord had somehow gotten wound around his ankle. He had taken only two steps when the cord tightened, tripping the heavy man and sending him sprawling over the front pew and into Mrs. Bowers' lap.

As two men pulled her father upright, Mitzi grabbed the microphone and proudly declared, "That's my dad!" Everyone (except the minister's wife) laughed so loudly that anyone who happened to be passing outside might have wondered what kind of church this was.

If they had asked her, Mitzi could have told them. It was a place that taught the most important things in life – love and caring! And the church's best teacher was her dad.

Father's Day was begun by
Mrs. John Bruce Dodd in
Spokane, Washington, in 1909.
After the death of his wife, her
father had raised a large family alone.
Mrs. Dodd honored him with a
special day to recognize his sacrifices.
In 1910 the entire city of Spokane
joined in the idea, and
by 1920 most Americans marked
the third Sunday in June as
Father's Day.